£6.00

GW00417565

Improve your scales!

A workbook for examinations

Flute Grades 1–3

Paul Harris

Contents

© 2000 by Faber Music Ltd
First published in 2000 by Faber Music Ltd
Bloomsbury House 74–77 Great Russell Street London WC1B 3DA
Printed in England by Caligraving Ltd
All rights reserved

ISBN10: 0-571-52024-3
EAN13: 978-0-571-52024-4

To buy Faber Music publications or to find out about the full range of titles available
please contact your local retailer or Faber Music sales enquiries:
Tel: +44 (0)1279 82 89 82   Fax: +44 (0)1279 82 89 83
sales@fabermusic.com   fabermusic.com

Introduction

To the student

Have you ever realised that it is much easier to learn something if you want to? Do you ever forget your telephone number? How many characters can you name from your favourite 'soap' or football team? Scales are not difficult to learn if you really want to learn them. Not only will they improve many aspects of your technique, but you will also get high marks in the scale section of grade exams, you will be able to learn pieces more quickly (difficult passages are often nothing more than scale patterns) and your sight-reading will improve too! Treat scales as friends – they will pay you great dividends!

To the teacher

Scales and arpeggios are often a real stumbling block for exam candidates and budding musicians. *Improve your scales!* is designed to make scale preparation and learning fun!

Working through the book will encourage your pupils to approach scales and arpeggios methodically and thoughtfully. It will help with memory problems and turn scale-learning into an enjoyable experience.

Simultaneous learning

Scales, sight-reading and aural are often the aspects of teaching relegated to the final few minutes of a lesson. The link between scales (particularly in the development of 'key-sense' and the recognition of melodic/harmonic patterns) and sight-reading is obvious, and there are many ways to integrate aural into the process too. Thus the use of the material in this book as a more central feature of a lesson is strongly recommended, especially when used in conjunction with *Improve your sight-reading!* Pupils will learn to become more musically aware, make fewer mistakes and allow the teacher to concentrate on teaching the music!

Using the book

The purpose of this workbook is to incorporate regular scale playing into lessons and daily practice and to help pupils prepare for grade examinations. You need not work at all sections, nor in the order as set out, but the best results may well be achieved by adhering fairly closely to the material.

Know the Notes! is to prove that the actual notes are known! Students should be encouraged to say the notes up and down until this can be done really fluently.

The **Finger Fitness** exercises are to strengthen the fingers and to cover technically tricky areas. They should be played legato, detached, staccato and any other form of mixed articulation that you can devise! When they are fluent you may like to add dynamic levels and vary the rhythmic patterns. Always encourage an active awareness of intonation. It is recommended that these exercises are played slowly until real control is achieved.

The **Scale Study** and **Arpeggio Study** are really extended exercises, but place the material in a more musical and 'fun' context. Some have *ad lib.* accompaniments or you might like to improvise a simple piano accompaniment; this would add interest and help the student with intonation and time.

Have a go is to encourage thought 'in the key', through the improvisation or composition of a short tune.

As a further exercise to develop the ability to think in a key, encourage pupils to play (by ear) a well known melody – for example, Happy Birthday or the National Anthem (major), 'Greensleeves' or 'God rest ye merry, gentlemen' (minor). You might like to ask pupils to improvise a simple variation on their chosen melody. This could be rhythmic or dynamic to begin. As they grow in confidence they might try 'decorating' the melody.

Say→Think→Play! is where the student finally plays the scale and arpeggio. The following method should really help in memorising each scale and arpeggio:

1 **Say** the notes out loud, up and down, and repeat until fluent.
2 Say the notes out loud and finger the scale. Don't proceed further until this can be done confidently and accurately.
3 **Think** the notes and finger the scale (but don't play out loud).
4 Think the notes and **play** the scale/arpeggio. By this time there should be no doubt in the player's mind and there should certainly be no fumbles or wrong notes!

Marking

A marking system has been included to help you and the student to monitor progress and to act as a means of encouragement. It is suggested you adopt a grading system as follows:

A Excellent work!
B Good work, but keep at it!
C A little more practice would be a good idea!
D No time to lose – get practising at once!

Revision

At the end of each stage you will find a **Revision Practice** table. As the new scales become more familiar you will wish your student to revise them regularly. This table is to encourage a methodical approach to scale practice, and show that there are endless ways of practising scales and arpeggios! Fill out the table for each week, or each practice session as follows:

1 Mark L for legato, D for detached and S for staccato, or;

2 Choose a different articulation pattern each time from the following:
Scales:

Arpeggios:

3 Choose a different rhythmic pattern each time from the following:

4 Finally, choose a different dynamic level. As students get into the habit of good scale and arpeggio practice they should no longer need the table.

Group Teaching

Improve your scales! is ideal for group teaching. Members of the group should be asked to comment on performances of the **Finger Fitness** exercises – was the tone even? Were the fingers moving rhythmically and together when necessary? Was the pulse even? *etc*. Exercises could be split between two or more players (for example, playing alternate phrases), and constructive criticism should be encouraged for the scale and arpeggio studies. With the optional *ad lib.* parts, a small group of the pieces could be performed at a private 'group concert', or even at a more formal concert.

F major 1 octave

Know the Notes!

1 Write the key signature of F major:

2 Write out the notes of the scale:

3 Write out the notes of the arpeggio:

Finger Fitness

Practise the **Finger Fitness** exercises very slowly at first and always practise them legato, detached and staccato (see Introduction).

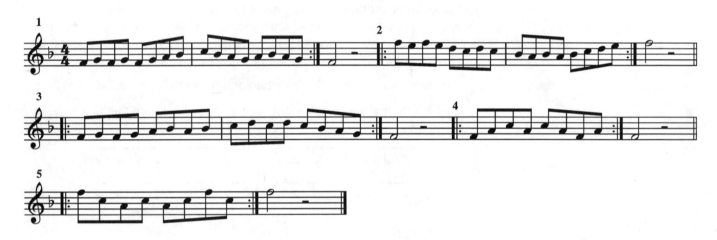

First and Fruity

Scale study in F major

Festive Fanfare

Arpeggio study in F major

Player 2
(ad lib.)

Have a go

Compose or improvise your own tune in F major. If you are writing your tune down, remember to put in some markings and then give your piece a title.

Say

Say the notes out loud, up and down, then say the notes out loud and finger the scale/arpeggio.

Think

Think the notes and finger the scale/arpeggio.

Play!

Play the scale and arpeggio.

Revision Practice

F major (1 octave)	1	2	3	4	5	6	7	8	9	10
Legato/Detached/Staccato										
Articulation pattern										
Rhythmic pattern										
Dynamic level										

Marking

F major (1 octave)	
Know the notes!	
Finger fitness	
Scale study	
Arpeggio study	
Have a go	
Say → think → play!	

F major 2 octaves

Finger Fitness

Fiendish Feet

Scale study in F major

Frogs Frolic

Arpeggio study in F major

Revision Practice

F major 2 octaves	1	2	3	4	5	6	7	8	9	10
Legato/Detached/Staccato										
Articulation pattern										
Rhythmic pattern										
Dynamic level										

Marking

F major 2 octaves	Grade
Finger fitness	
Scale study	
Arpeggio study	
Say→think→play!	

Revise **Finger Fitness** exercises on page 4 for the lower octave.

Don't forget to **Have a go** at improvising or composing a piece using the full two-octave range.

G major 1 octave

Know the Notes!

1 Write the key signature of G major:

2 Write out the notes of the scale:

3 Write out the notes of the arpeggio:

Finger Fitness

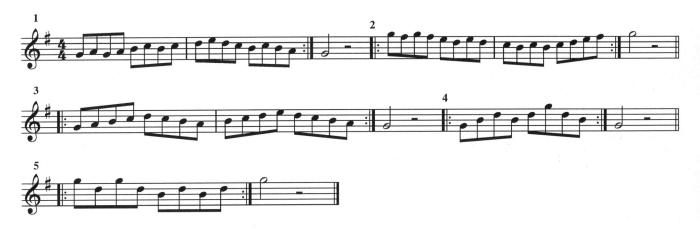

Gremlins

Scale study in G major

Galloping Galoshes

Arpeggio study in G major

Allegretto con moto

Have a go

Compose or improvise your own tune in G major.

Say
Think
Play!

Say the notes out loud, up and down, then say the notes out loud and finger the scale/arpeggio.

Think the notes and finger the scale/arpeggio.

Play the scale and arpeggio.

Revision Practice

G major (1 octave)	1	2	3	4	5	6	7	8	9	10
Legato/Detached/Staccato										
Articulation pattern										
Rhythmic pattern										
Dynamic level										

Marking

G major (1 octave)	Grade
Know the notes!	
Finger fitness	
Scale study	
Arpeggio study	
Have a go	
Say → think → play!	

G major 2 octaves

Finger Fitness

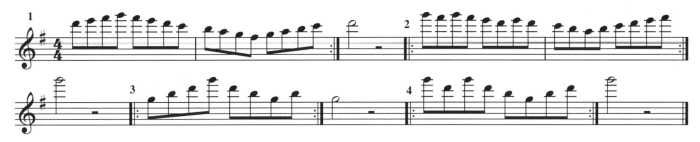

Gabbling Geese
Scale study in G major

Giraffe
Arpeggio study in G major

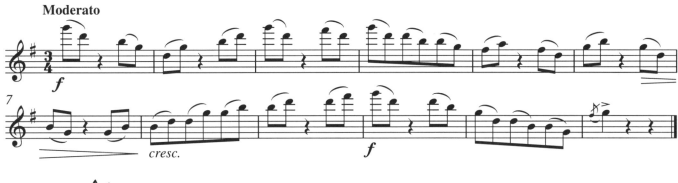

Player 2
(ad lib.)

Revision Practice

G major 2 octaves	1	2	3	4	5	6	7	8	9	10
Legato/Detached/Staccato										
Articulation pattern										
Rhythmic pattern										
Dynamic level										

Marking

G major 2 octaves	Grade
Finger fitness	
Scale study	
Arpeggio study	
Say→think→play!	

Revise **Finger Fitness** exercises on page 7 for the lower octave.

Don't forget to **Have a go** at improvising or composing a piece using the full two-octave range.

E harmonic minor 1 octave

Know the Notes!

1 Write the key signature of E minor:

2 Write out the notes of the scale:

3 Write out the notes of the arpeggio:

Finger Fitness

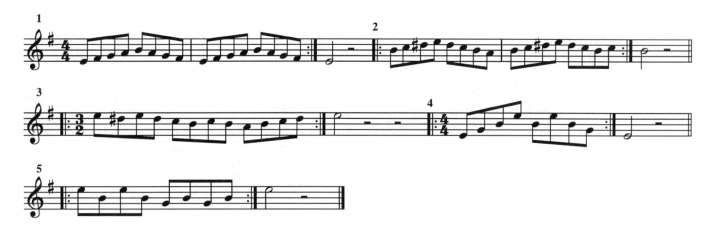

Eastern Elegy

Scale study in E harmonic minor

Escalator

Arpeggio study in E minor

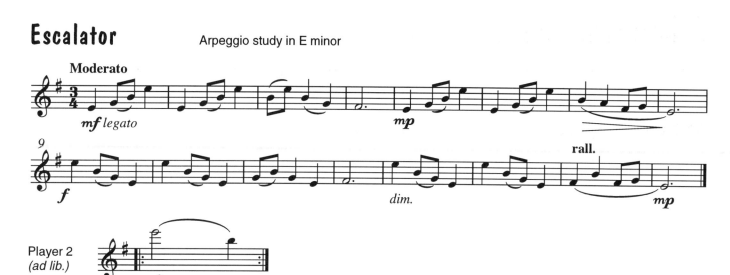

Have a go

Compose or improvise your own tune using the notes of E harmonic minor.

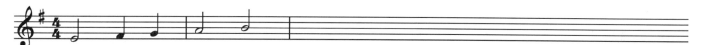

Say
Think
Play!

Say the notes out loud, up and down, then say the notes out loud and finger the scale/arpeggio.

Think the notes and finger the scale/arpeggio.

Play the scale and arpeggio.

Revision Practice

E harmonic minor (1 octave)	1	2	3	4	5	6	7	8	9	10
Legato/Detached/Staccato										
Articulation pattern										
Rhythmic pattern										
Dynamic level										

Marking

E harmonic minor (1 octave)	Grade
Know the notes!	
Finger fitness	
Scale study	
Arpeggio study	
Have a go	
Say → think → play!	

E melodic minor 1 octave

Know the Notes!

1 Write the key signature of E minor:

2 Write out the notes of the scale:

up→						
						←down

3 Write out the notes of the arpeggio:

Finger Fitness

Easter Egg

Scale study in E melodic minor

Exams are Extremely Enjoyable!

Arpeggio study in E minor

Allegro con spirito

Have a go

Compose or improvise your own tune using the notes of E melodic minor.

Say

Think

Play!

Say the notes out loud, up and down, then say the notes out loud and finger the scale/arpeggio.

Think the notes and finger the scale/arpeggio.

Play the scale and arpeggio.

Revision Practice

E melodic minor (1 octave)	1	2	3	4	5	6	7	8	9	10
Legato/Detached/Staccato										
Articulation pattern										
Rhythmic pattern										
Dynamic level										

Marking

E melodic minor (1 octave)	Grade
Know the notes!	
Finger fitness	
Scale study	
Arpeggio study	
Have a go	
Say → think → play!	

14

E minor 2 octaves

Finger Fitness

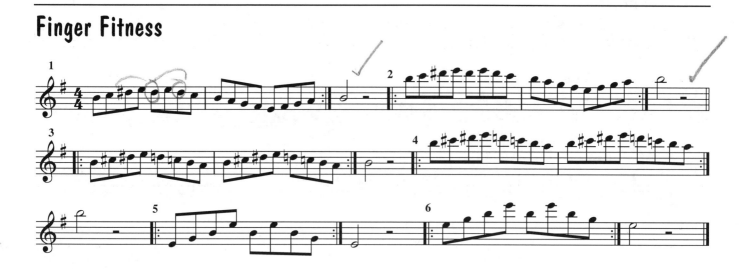

Eccentric Elephant

Scale study in E harmonic minor

Elizabethan Elegy

Scale study in E melodic minor

Elegant Eclair

Arpeggio study in E minor

Say

Say the notes out loud, up and down, then say the notes out loud and finger the scale/arpeggio.

Think

Think the notes and finger the scale/arpeggio.

Play!

Play the scale and arpeggio.

Revision Practice

E minor 2 octaves	1	2	3	4	5	6	7	8	9	10
Harmonic/Melodic										
Legato/Detached/Staccato										
Articulation pattern										
Rhythmic pattern										
Dynamic level										

Marking

E minor 2 octaves	Grade
Finger fitness	
Scale study (harmonic)	
Scale study (melodic)	
Arpeggio study	
Say→think→play!	

Revise **Finger Fitness** exercises on pages 10 and 12 for the lower octave.

Don't forget to **Have a go** at improvising or composing a piece using the full two-octave range.

A minor   1 octave

Know the Notes!

1 Write the key signature of A minor:

2 Write out the notes of the harmonic scale:

3 Write out the notes of the melodic scale:

up→							
							←down

4 Write out the notes of the arpeggio:

Finger Fitness

Arabian Apricot   Scale study in A harmonic minor

Acorn Aria

Scale study in A melodic minor

Armadillo

Arpeggio study in A minor

Have a go

Compose or improvise your own tune using the notes of A harmonic minor.

18

Have another go Compose or improvise your own tune using the notes of A melodic minor.

Say
Think
Play!

Say the notes out loud, up and down, then say the notes out loud and finger the scale/arpeggio.

Think the notes and finger the scale/arpeggio.

Play the scale and arpeggio

Revision Practice

A minor (1 octave)	1	2	3	4	5	6	7	8	9	10
Harmonic/Melodic										
Legato/Detached/Staccato										
Articulation pattern										
Rhythmic pattern										
Dynamic level										

Marking

A minor (1 octave)	Grade
Know the notes!	
Finger fitness	
Scale study (harmonic)	
Scale study (melodic)	
Arpeggio study	
Have a go	
Have another go	
Say → think → play!	

A minor 12th

Finger Fitness

Amorous Anchovy

Scale study in A harmonic minor

Ants

Scale study in A melodic minor

Aviary *fairly fast*

Arpeggio study in A minor

Allegretto grazioso — *gracefully.*

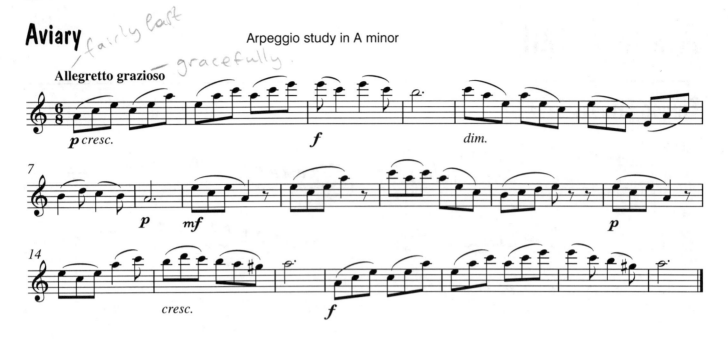

Say

Say the notes out loud, up and down, then say the notes out loud and finger the scale/arpeggio.

Think

Think the notes and finger the scale/arpeggio.

Play!

Play the scale and arpeggio.

Revision Practice

A minor 12th	1	2	3	4	5	6	7	8	9	10
Harmonic/Melodic										
Legato/Detached/Staccato										
Articulation pattern										
Rhythmic pattern										
Dynamic level										

Marking

A minor 12th	Grade
Finger fitness	
Scale study (harmonic)	
Scale study (melodic)	
Arpeggio study	
Say→think→play!	

Revise **Finger Fitness** exercises on page 16 for the lower octave.

Don't forget to **Have a go** at improvising or composing a piece using the range of a twelfth.

Bb major 12th

Know the Notes!

1 Write the key signature of B♭ major:

2 Write out the notes of the scale:

3 Write out the notes of the arpeggio:

Finger Fitness

Boiled Beef

Scale study in B♭ major

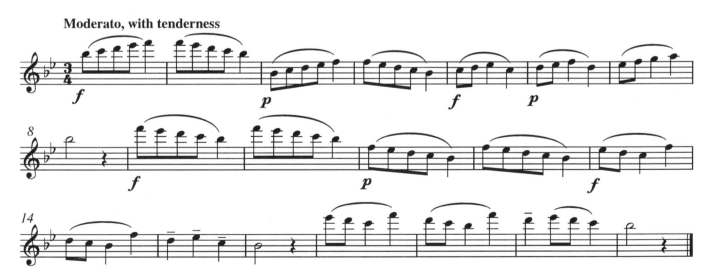

Brontasaurus

Arpeggio study in B♭ major

Have a go

Compose or improvise your own tune in B♭ major.

Say
Think
Play!

Say the notes out loud, up and down, then say the notes out loud and finger the scale/arpeggio.

Think the notes and finger the scale/arpeggio.

Play the scale and arpeggio.

Revision Practice

B♭ major 12th	1	2	3	4	5	6	7	8	9	10
Legato/Detached/Staccato										
Articulation pattern										
Rhythmic pattern										
Dynamic level										

Marking

B♭ major 12th	Grade
Know the notes!	
Finger fitness	
Scale study	
Arpeggio study	
Have a go	
Say → think → play!	

D major 2 octaves

Know the Notes!

1 Write the key signature of D major:

2 Write out the notes of the scale:

3 Write out the notes of the arpeggio:

Finger Fitness

Dotty Ditty

Scale study in D major

Ding-dong Drone Arpeggio study in D major

f like the sound of bells

Have a go

Compose or improvise your own tune in D major.

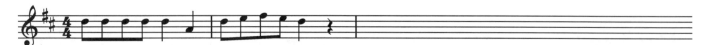

Say
Think
Play!

Say the notes out loud, up and down, then say the notes out loud and finger the scale/arpeggio.

Think the notes and finger the scale/arpeggio.

Play the scale and arpeggio.

Revision Practice

D major (2 octaves)	1	2	3	4	5	6	7	8	9	10
Legato/Detached/Staccato										
Articulation pattern										
Rhythmic pattern										
Dynamic level										

Marking

D major (2 octaves)	Grade
Know the notes!	
Finger fitness	
Scale study	
Arpeggio study	
Have a go	
Say → think → play!	

D minor 2 octaves

Know the Notes!

1 Write the key signature of D minor:

2 Write out the notes of the harmonic scale:

3 Write out the notes of the melodic scale:

up →						
						←down

4 Write out the notes of the arpeggio:

Finger Fitness

Doleful Dolphin   Scale study in D harmonic minor

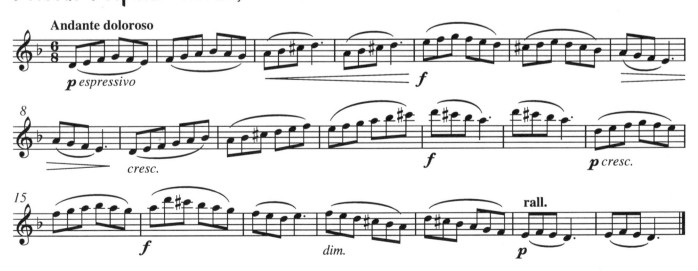

Dizzy Donkey

Scale study in D melodic minor

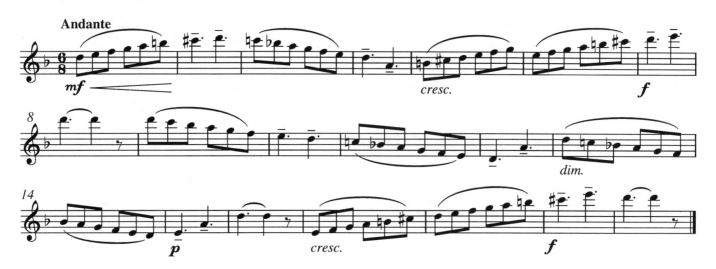

Duet

Arpeggio study in D minor

The second player starts at the beginning, one beat after the first player

Have a go

Compose or improvise your own tune using the notes of D harmonic minor.

Have another go
Compose or improvise your own tune using the notes of D melodic minor.

Say
Think
Play!

Say the notes out loud, up and down, then say the notes out loud and finger the scale/arpeggio.

Think the notes and finger the scale/arpeggio.

Play the scale and arpeggio.

Revision Practice

D minor 2 octaves	1	2	3	4	5	6	7	8	9	10
Harmonic/Melodic										
Legato/Detached/Staccato										
Articulation pattern										
Rhythmic pattern										
Dynamic level										

Marking

D minor 2 octaves	Grade
Know the notes!	
Finger fitness	
Scale study (harmonic)	
Scale study (melodic)	
Arpeggio study	
Have a go	
Have another go	
Say → think → play!	

G minor 2 octaves

Know the Notes!

1 Write the key signature of G minor:

2 Write out the notes of the harmonic scale:

3 Write out the notes of the melodic scale:

up →					
					←down

4 Write out the notes of the arpeggio:

Finger Fitness

Graceful Ghost   Scale study in G harmonic minor

Grumpy

Scale study in G melodic minor

Gruesome Gravy

Arpeggio study in G minor

Player 2
(ad lib.)

Have a go

Compose or improvise your own tune using the notes of G harmonic minor.

Have another go

Compose or improvise your own tune using the notes of G melodic minor.

Say

   Think

      Play!

Say the notes out loud, up and down, then say the notes out loud and finger the scale/arpeggio.

Think the notes and finger the scale/arpeggio.

Play the scale and arpeggio.

Revision Practice

G minor 2 octaves	1	2	3	4	5	6	7	8	9	10
Harmonic/Melodic										
Legato/Detached/Staccato										
Articulation pattern										
Rhythmic pattern										
Dynamic level										

Marking

G minor 2 octaves	Grade
Know the notes!	
Finger fitness	
Scale study (harmonic)	
Scale study (melodic)	
Arpeggio study	
Have a go	
Have another go	
Say → think → play!	

Performance tips

1   Always play scales and arpeggios with your best tone quality.

2   Tone quality must be as even as possible throughout.

3   Don't land on the last note with a 'bump'.

4   Finger movement should always be firm and precise.

5   Rhythm must be even, and pulse steady throughout.

6   Make sure all notes are of equal duration in tongued scales and arpeggios.

7   Don't change tempo or lose rhythmic control when you change direction.

8   Don't accent the top note.

9   Always play scales carefully in tune.

10   Make sure that your finger movement is well co-ordinated in arpeggios.

11   At exams, play all scales at the same tempo and about mezzo-forte (*mf*).

12   Remember that scales *are* music; play each one with shape and direction.

Scales and arpeggios

SCALES AND ARPEGGIOS (exam requirements of the Associated Board)
From memory, to be played both slurred and tongued in the indicated keys for each Grade:
GRADE 1: F, G majors (one octave); E minor (one octave); E, A minors (one octave)*
GRADE 2: F, G majors (one octave); D major (two octaves); E, A minors (one octave)*
GRADE 3: Bb major (a twelfth); D, F, G majors (two octaves); A minor (a twelfth); D, E, G minors (two octaves)*
Chromatic Scale: starting on F (one octave)
*Scales: in the above keys (minors in melodic *or* harmonic form at candidate's choice)
Arpeggios: the common chords of the above keys for the range indicated.

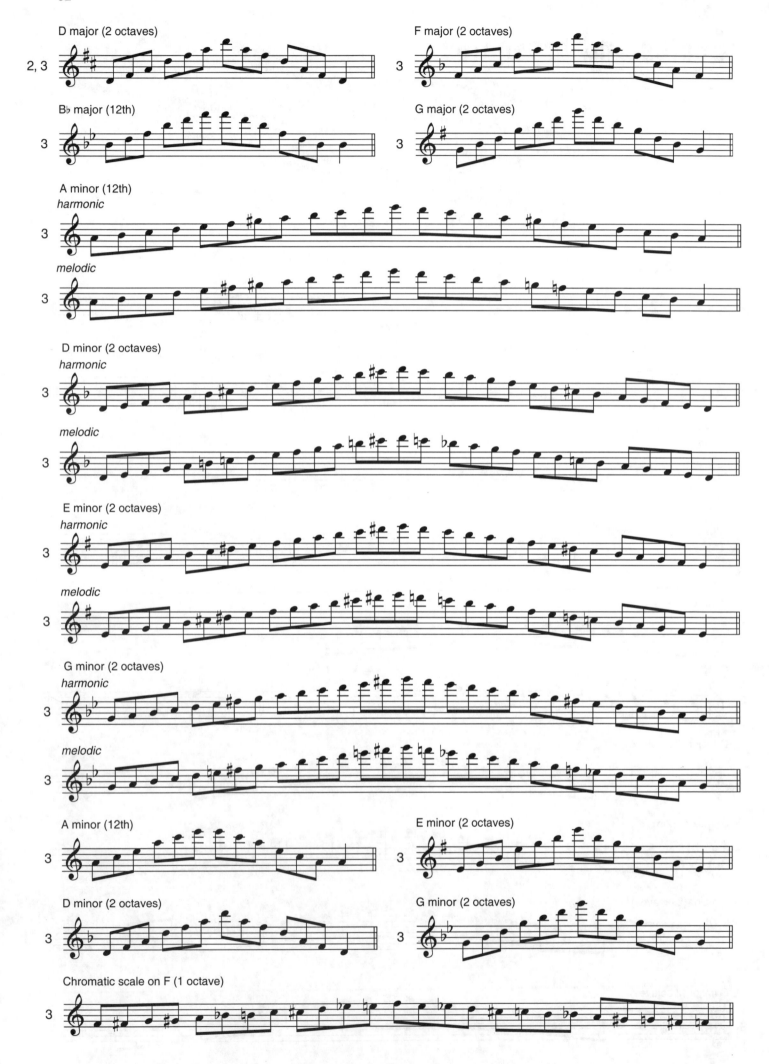